The Place of

Jane Spiro

Series Editor: John McRae

Edward Arnold
A division of Hodder & Stoughton
LONDON   MELBOURNE   AUCKLAND

© 1990 Jane Spiro

First published in Great Britain 1990

British Library Cataloguing in Publication Data

Spiro, Jane
  The place of the lotus. – (Edward Arnold readers library).
  1. English language – Readers
  I. Title
  428.6

  ISBN 0–340–52639–4

Typeset in 12/14 pt Times by Colset Private Limited, Singapore
Printed and bound in Great Britain for Edward Arnold, the educational, academic and medical publishing division of Hodder and Stoughton Limited, Mill Road, Dunton Green, Sevenoaks, Kent, by Cambus Litho, East Kilbride

Chapter 1

The Place of the Lotus

The lotus is a large flower that swims on the water. It is found in lakes that are not deep. Large gardens of lotus flowers swim together in lakes and rivers. Their leaves are pink and white, and as large as plates.

The lotus is a special flower.

Firstly, it is special because it is as round as the earth. It is a perfect circle. An Indian story tells us that the god Brahma stood on a lotus flower. He stood at the centre of the lotus circle. Then he looked north, south, east, and west before making the world. Another story tells us about Buddha. When Buddha was born, a lotus flower opened out. Buddha stepped into the circle. He looked all around the circle in ten directions. In this way, he could think about all parts of the earth.

Secondly, the lotus is special because it grows in water. Many peoples believed water was the beginning of life. For the Egyptians, the Nile was the place of fertility – the beginning of life. The lotus, too, was the beginning of life: it grew in the waters of the Nile.

The stories in this book are about earth and water and the relationship between them.

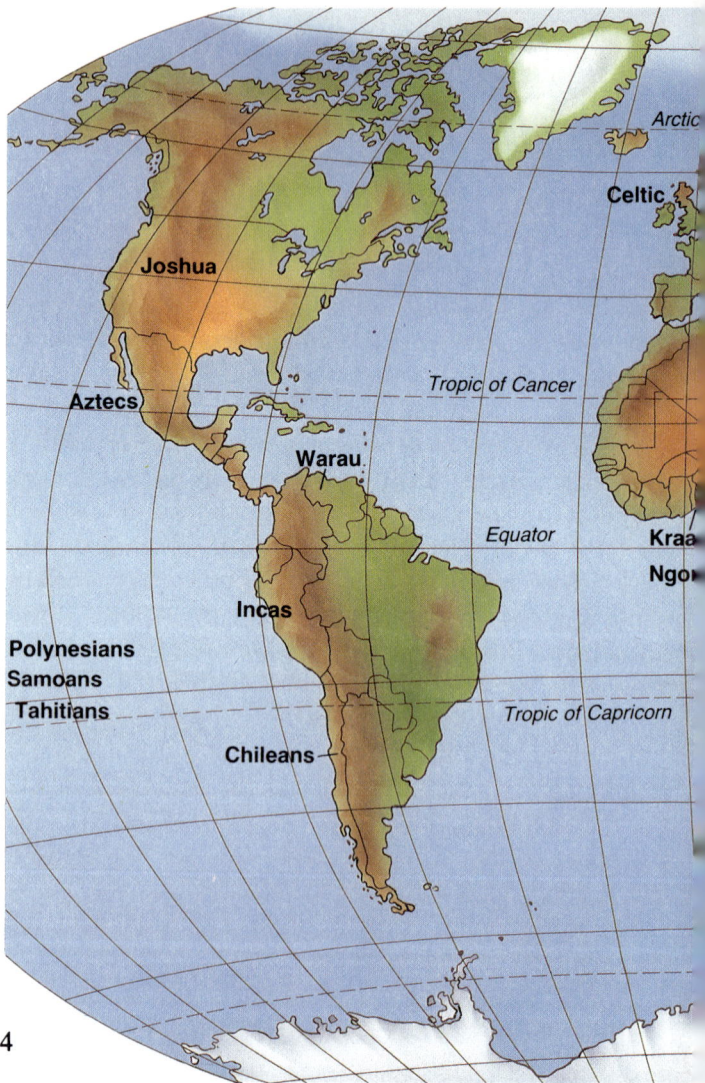

Arctic

Celtic

Joshua

Aztecs

Tropic of Cancer

Warau

Equator

Kraa

Ngo

Incas

Polynesians
Samoans
Tahitians

Tropic of Capricorn

Chileans

4

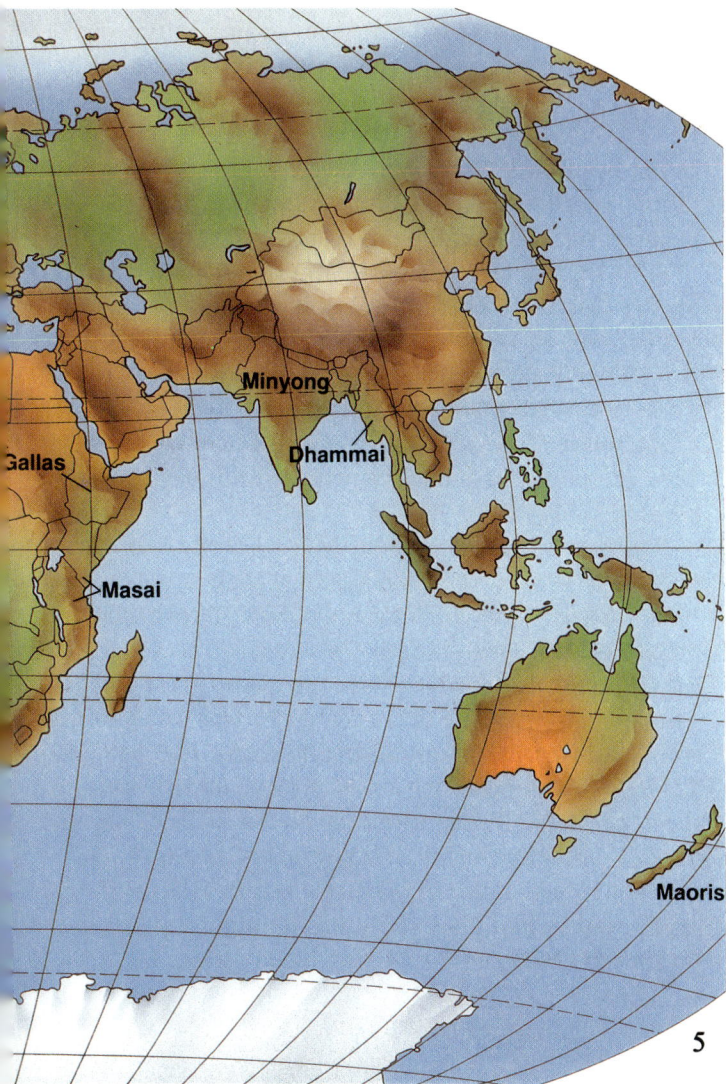

Gallas

Minyong

Dhammai

Masai

Maoris

5

Which came first? How did they begin? Is there a place in between earth and water? Can people live in both places?

In the beginning there was water
Many peoples believed that water came first. They believed that earth came out of the water.

The Middle Eastern Bible tells us that there were waters on the first day. The earth was made only on the third day. It was made when the waters moved and left dry land. The North American people tell the story of a small water rat who made earth from the waters. The rat brought one piece of sand from the bottom of the water. This piece of sand became bigger and bigger until it became land.

There are many ideas about who made the earth. Many peoples believe earth was made by a Maker, a Giver or a first Mover. The Joshua people of North America believed earth was made by Xowalaci, the Giver. The Masai people believed it was made by the great god Ngai who lived in the sky. Others thought it was small animals who made earth, or an ordinary man. The people of Tahiti, for example, tell us of a workman. He made a sheet of sand. Then he made the sand hold together strongly, by planting in it thousands of plants.

What is earth made of? Different stories tell us of mud, sand, rocks, dry land; of earth brought up from the bottom of the sea.

6

The separation of Earth and Sky

Many stories tell us of a time when Earth and Sky were joined together. Most of these stories come from countries with strong sunshine, for example, countries in Africa and South East Asia, where the sky seems very near. The stories tell us how uncomfortable it was for people. They lived in so small a place; there was no room for light or air. They have stories, too, of how Earth and Sky were separated. The Minyong Indians tell of a man, Sedi-Diyar. He caught the sky, and hit it until it escaped into the heavens. The Krachi people of Africa tell us about an old woman. She was beating flour with a wooden spoon. Every time she beat the flour, she beat the sky too. Sky had to escape higher and higher to be safe.

How people came to Earth

At first, people did not live on Earth. Maybe the Earth was not yet finished or maybe it was a place for animals only. Every race or tribe, nation or people, has a different story.

One story is that people lived in the sky first of all. The Dhammai Indians describe the first people in the sky. They become tired because they have nowhere to put their feet. Their children fall down; bad animals eat them. For that reason, the father builds an earth for the children to live safely. Another story is that the first people lived in a Heaven. The Earth is a place of punishment. In the Bible story, Adam and Eve lived in a beautiful garden. When

7

they break their promise, and eat the apple, they must leave the garden. Then they go and live on Earth; they take bad with them. The Ngombe people of Africa have a similar story. All people lived in heaven at first. One old woman, Mbokumu, made the Maker angry. He sent her to earth in a basket as a punishment.

How Death came to Earth

In the beginning people lived forever. All the stories tell us this. They tell us that Death was a punishment. It came to Earth because a man or woman broke a promise. Eve ate the apple, Pandora opened the box full of bad things.

Not all the stories blame women, however. The Gallas people of Africa say it was a bird who gave Death to mankind. The bird had a message to give people. 'You will live forever. When you are old, you must change your skin. Then you will be young again.' But the bird changed the message. He wanted meat from a snake. So he told the snake: 'You will live forever. You will change your skin. But men will die.'

A Buddhist tale tells us that Death was brought to Earth by three brothers. They found a pot of gold. The brothers were so greedy that each wanted the gold for himself alone. They each tried to kill the other. In the end Death took the gold for himself.

The great flood

The Bible tells us of a great flood. Almost everyone died

8

in this flood. The family of Noah alone was saved. This story is not only Middle Eastern. In fact, we find the story in so many continents, north, south, east and west. We must ask ourselves: did this flood really happen?

The people of the lower Congo tell of a flood: the whole village died, the people and all their animals. The people of Chile, the Aztecs of Mexico, the Incas of Peru tell of a flood. On the other side of the world, the people of Samoa tell of a flood. These stories have many ideas which are the same.

Firstly, they tell us of one or two people who lived after the flood. These were often ordinary people – there was nothing unusual about them. Noah was an ordinary person. So are the man and woman in the Aztec story, Coxcotli and Xochiquetzal. But they are the people who make new life. The people who live sometimes escape in a boat, like Noah. Others escape by climbing a high mountain, like the man in the Inca story. They escape because they are practical, not because they are extraordinary.

Secondly, the end of the flood is a beginning. The stories tell us about new people who are made, new islands, new languages. A small bird brings new languages to the Aztec people. It is another bird, the dove, that comes to Noah. The dove tells Noah that the flood is finished.

Water here is a punishment. People are washed away in the flood stories. Often they come back better, or different.

Magic islands

Water is a place where life begins. It is also a place of death and punishment. For this reason, islands are very special places. They are neither land nor sea, but something mysterious in between.

Many stories tell us about the mystery of islands. There are islands under the sea, like Atlantis. There are islands where people travel after death, like Avalon. King Arthur, in the Celtic story, travelled to Avalon after death. Morgan la Fay, priestess of water, travelled with him in the boat.

The Celts tell stories of sea-travellers, like Mael Duin. Their journeys are filled with strange dream-islands, islands made of gold, or made from a giant foot.

In many of these stories, the traveller never returns. The island is a place that separates him forever from his home. Once the traveller enters the dream, he can never leave it.

Chapter 2

In the Beginning there was Water
The Separation of Earth and Water

A myth of the North American Joshua people

The man with the black eyes smoked tobacco. It made a small cloud of smoke in the room. The room was small and silent. It had large windows and walls of grass and wood.

'What can you see through that window?' the man asked his companion, and blew another cloud of smoke into the room.

'Water,' said his companion. 'All around, water. What more is there to see?'

Water spread like a mirror all around. Water closed in around the walls of the house. Water moved out in the distance until it met the sky.

'You haven't done a very good job. There's nothing much around here. Only cloud and water. What kind of world is that?'

'Don't worry me now,' said the man with the tobacco. 'I'm working.'

The house sat on the water like a bird. And all around there was cloud. The man with the black eyes smoked. He smoked, and sat, and worked. His companion walked up and down, up and down.

'This place is too small,' he said. 'Can't you make something bigger?'

But Xowalaci the Giver said nothing. He only made clouds of smoke.

'You say you are the Giver. You bring me here to help you give. But what? To whom? Nothing happens here. There is nothing to do, and no-one to talk to. I've had enough, do you hear? I'm going.'

'Of course you may go. But where will you go to?'

First Man opened the door. Water all around. A flat mirror of water. Water closing in to the walls of the house. Water moving out to meet the sky.

'Out there. I'll go out there,' said First Man.

And then something strange happened. The clouds moved. A crack of light appeared. It hit the water and made it burst into colour. A wide red path of fire broke through the clouds.

'Oh Xowalaci, Giver, something marvellous is happening!' shouted First Man. He ran into the house.

'I am working,' the Giver said. 'Don't worry me.' And he made rings of smoke with his tobacco.

First Man ran to the door. Something else was happening. The line of the water seemed to be moving nearer. The water was breaking into waves. The clouds were lifting. The line was moving, nearer and nearer. As it moved, First Man saw two dark lines.

'Trees! Trees!' he cried. 'Giver, land is coming!'

'I'm working,' said the Giver. He sat quietly, and made rings of smoke.

First Man stood and watched. The land moved towards him. The trees became clearer and clearer. Their lines were sharp and black. And the land moved like a fall of snow. Nearer and nearer.

'It's white. The land is white. Is that right, Giver?'

'I'm still working,' said the Giver. 'The work is not finished.'

Land pushed through the water. The water broke and parted. The trees moved nearer. Their lines became wider, darker. First Man could see branches – thin lines like fingers. And then land closed in. A white carpet lay all around the house.

'It's here! The land has arrived!'

'Stand on the land. Is it strong like wood? Or is it soft like grass?'

First Man took one step.

'Soft like grass,' he said.

'Then the work is not finished.'

The Giver moved to the door. He blew rings of smoke across the land.

'First Man, how would you like the world to be?'

'I would like more colours, Giver. White is very boring.'

'What else?'

'I would like things to grow. Everything is so still here. I

14

want things to grow, move.'

'I see. What else?'

'I would like more land. This piece of land is too small. I want land wherever I look. I want land so that I can walk for days.'

'I see. You ask for very little. What else?'

'I want people who are the same as me. I want companions who ask questions, like me.'

'I see. And what else?'

'I want land and sea to be friends so that the water does not fight the land and the land does not fight the water.'

'I am working.' The Giver made five rings of smoke, one for each answer. They blew across the land.

The Giver walked round and round the piece of land. Night and day he walked. He walked, and smoked. Light came, light went. And now it was First Man who stayed in the house.

'Wait for me,' the Giver said. 'I must work alone.'

Then grass pushed through the white earth. New trees pushed through. Leaves opened on the branches. The snow-world became green with plants, trees and flowers.

The water around the land jumped and boiled. The sea was angry.

'Move away,' shouted the Giver. 'This is the place of the land. There is plenty of room for you in other places.'

The sea was grey with anger. But it fell back, leaving a line of wet sand across the land.

'I have made the land green. I have made plants grow.

The sea now falls back, and leaves the land in peace. But the land is still too small. Now I must make the land grow.'

He made a cake of mud with his hands. He dropped it in the water. For many minutes he waited. At last there was a 'plop' – very very quiet, very very far away.

'Cake of mud, find another cake. Join together. Cake find cake. Make a chain of mud.'

Mud joined mud joined mud. A chain of mud. Then he dropped a stone into the water. He waited – then 'plop'; a little sooner, a little louder, a little nearer. He waited.

And then, he dropped a third stone. This time – 'plop' – it fell, clear and loud; it touched the bottom, the land.

The water broke away in tall waves, from north, south, west, east, water fell away; waves as high as houses climbed the sea. And the land lifted out of the water like the back of a great animal.

'First Man, look at this! Come here! Look what I have done!'

The land opened out all the way to the sky. It spread flat and yellow, a beach without end. The two of them stood by the door of the hut. They looked, silently.

'Wait, there is something here I don't like,' said the Giver.

There was a line in the sand: a deep line burned from north to south of the endless beach. They looked, silently. The clouds moved across the sand. Then the Giver said, sick at heart,

17

'They are footprints.'

'That is not possible,' said First Man.

'It is not possible. But that is what they are.' First Man looked. His eyes hurt with looking. The footprints laughed at him.

'But I am the First Man,' he said quietly.

'And I am the First Giver,' said the First Giver.

He covered land again with water. And then washed it dry. The land lifted out of the water. This time the steps marked the land from west to east. Four times the Giver washed the land. And each time the steps burned across the land like a strange smile.

First Man and First Giver stood on their doorstep. They were alone in the new world.

'Someone else is here,' said First Man.

'Someone walked on the bed of the sea, before I gave the sea a bed,' said the First Giver.

They watched the wind run over the sand. Each step was a deep dark bowl. Each step laughed at them.

'There is something about this I don't like,' said Xowalaci, the Giver.

And the waves washed over the land.

Chapter 3

The Separation of Earth and Sky

A myth of the Maori people of New Zealand

At one time, people lived in a long dark tunnel. They grew taller in the long tunnel, then they hit their heads on the roof and grew no more. Trees grew in the tunnel but they grew thin and small without the light. Birds flew, but very, very low. And sometimes the tunnel's roof was so low that people had to crawl on the ground, like snakes.

Earth and sky were too close. They were so close, there was no room for people.

'I am Rangi, roof of the world. I wrap like a ball of wool around the earth. The earth sits in the palm of my hand.'

'I am Papatua, the Earth. The sky wraps around me like a vine around a tree; a circle within a circle.'

This did not please the earth-people.

'But what about us?' cried one. 'Because of your love there is no room for us. There is no room for the light. No room for trees to grow. No room for birds to fly.'

'Because of you I must bend my head when I walk!'

'Because of you I can see nothing. I cannot see my children. I cannot see the trees!'

'What selfish love is this?' shouted Kiri. 'So you can be close, all of us must suffer. Can love like this be good?'

Papatua was angry. Her mountains smoked, her rivers boiled.

'Egg and yolk cannot be separated. Fruit and stone cannot be separated. Body and heart cannot be separated. So we cannot be separated.'

Sky held the Earth closer and closer. The earth-people had so little room, they could hardly breathe. They had no light, no air.

So one day, the earth-people called a meeting.

Hundreds came to the meeting. They sat low on the ground: it was a carpet of people.

'We are here to ask one question!' shouted Kiri. 'We need more room. We need to separate Earth and Sky. How can we do it?'

'Tell Earth and Sky we will find another home unless they separate. We cannot live like this, like snakes in the grass,' said one.

'No, no. Earth and Sky will only laugh and say "Go then. Find another home." That is no answer.'

'We must stop Sky loving Earth so much. We must make Earth ugly and angry. We must make her mountains smoke and her rivers boil. Then Sky will run away,' said another.

'No, no. Then our lives too will be difficult. If the Earth is ugly and angry, we too will suffer.'

20

There were many ideas. But none were quite right. None were the answer. Then, at last, one earth-man stood up.

'We cannot change the love between Earth and Sky. They will never choose to separate. Not even for us, their children, will they separate. So we must separate them ourselves. We must use all our strength, to lift the roof of the world.'

The earth-people listened to this.

'Are we strong enough?'

'Are there enough of us?'

'Are we brave enough?'

'Yes!' cried one.

'Yes!' cried another.

There was a chorus of voices. 'Yes! Yes! That is what we will do!' they shouted.

They chose a time when Earth was sleeping. There was no wind. The trees and rivers were still. The birds were quiet. Sky was so dark and low that it sat on their backs like a heavy dark stone. In the dark, the people met. First Kiri and his family. Then Kaora his friend, with his family. Then from the trees another group and in the dark ten more faces. And another group came from the mountains; fifty more from the river village; another ten, twenty from the sea. The whites of their eyes everywhere came quietly together. They moved without words like cats.

'We must make a long line around the Earth,' Kiri said.

What he said carried round the people like fire.

'We must cover every inch of the Earth. And when I lift my arms, every person must lift their arms. Push away the heavy stone that sits on our shoulders.'

The people made a circle around the earth. The Sky sat on their shoulders like a stone. They waited in the dark, like hundreds and hundreds of leaves, closed before the spring. And then, at last, from the centre of the Earth, 'Ahoi!' cried Kiri. He lifted his arms and pushed.

Like a thousand trees opening in spring, their hands opened: hand by hand opening out. A path of arms. As one person they pushed. Pushed, pushed the stone of the sky. Pushed until, with a great groan, the stone lifted. And a crack of light broke across the Earth.

'More! More! Push more!'

The crack of light became a wide river of light and it ran across the Earth and touched everything. Flowers opened. Birds began to sing.

'Look what an Earth there is!'

'Look what darkness has hidden for so long!'

They lifted the sky until it reached the mountain tops. The earth-people took away their arms. And there the sky stayed, hanging on the mountain tops like a great sheet.

Then Sky woke up. He felt cold and strange. He tried to touch the Earth.

'What! Earth has gone! She has left me!' He tried to turn over, but could not.

'What! I cannot move!' He tried to stretch himself.

'Help! Something hurts me, like a thousand needles!'
And then he looked down to Earth.

'Oh Earth where am I? You are suddenly so small, so far away! What has happened to me?'

'Sky, we have done this. We have separated you from Earth. Before, we were dying without air or light. We have separated you, so there is air between you.'

'Forgive us, Sky. We can all live better this way. When you and Earth are too close, it kills us.'

'The Earth will breathe better now.'

'We will breathe better now.'

'You will see the Earth better now. There is light for you to see her. You will know her better; love her better!'

The Sky looked down on the Earth. He wept large tears. They rained down on the grass and trees. The birds flew higher. The trees grew taller. The people walked with heads high.

'It is true. I see her better. I know her better. I love her better. Separation has done this to me.'

His tears make the rivers run faster.

Chapter 4

How People Came to Earth

A myth of the Warau people of the Caribbean

Man's first home was pleasant enough. It was a place in the sky – a place of cold air and cloud. It was a place close to the light of sun and moon: fire-red in the morning and blind-black at night. Though it was a quiet place, people were happy enough. They had never seen trees, running rivers or fields of moving grass, so they did not miss them.

Birds came to visit the people of the sky. Every bird was different. Every bird had different colours on its head and back; different shapes of wings and feet; some had lines of tall hairs on their heads; others had long tails like a brush. And every bird had a different song. They would stay a day or two. Then they would fly away. Many never came back again.

'Where do you come from?' Okohorote thought. 'And where do you go to? Is there another world, maybe? Is there another place where people walk and birds fly?'

One day Okohorote was walking through the sky. It was light to walk – like sitting in the movement of the sea. The air carried him. Suddenly, a bird cut the air. It moved like tongues of fire. Its head and back were red and the backs of its wings were blue as midnight.

'This one is a beauty,' thought Okohorote.

And then a new thought came to him.

'I will have it. I will keep it. I will find its home.'

He lifted from a passing cloud a hailstone as big as his hand; then he threw it with all his weight at the bird. The stone carried like an arrow in the air. It met the bird in the middle of flight. Bird and stone pulled down. Bird became stone, plunging through the air.

Okohorote watched, full of shame.

'What have I done?' he cried.

The bird fell like dying fire. It seemed that the bird pulled the sky down with it; a dark path burnt across the sky. And then the bird disappeared, plunging through a great burning hole to nowhere.

Okohorote could not move. The sight filled him with terror. The sky was hot with the fire of the bird and a dark hole now broke the sky in two.

He let the air carry him forward. It pulled him towards the hole. His curiosity pulled him there. The hole dropped down, it seemed forever. There was no end to it.

And at the bottom, small as a child's toy, was a garden. It was a new colour. A colour Okohorote did not know. Green.

The hole was wide enough to climb down. With his back on one side, Okohorote walked his way down. His feet walked the side of the tunnel. And so he dropped down – down – down. The green below came nearer and

26

nearer. He could see moving lines and colours. And then his feet touched a new ground. It was strong, hard ground. He touched it. Picked up a piece of it. Then he ran on it. Ran and ran. He ran into forests with tall trees and thick grass. He ran beside rivers falling over rocks. He ran through fields of high corn.

'This is where the birds live!' he cried. 'This is the world the birds return to. This is why they leave us and never come back.'

Every touch, every sound, every smell was new. And every movement was new. The snakes moved like a river in the grass. The monkeys jumped and danced in the trees. Wild cats sat under bushes and slept.

Four legs! Two legs! No legs! Okohorote's eyes were like plates. But the day was hot. Okohorote's work had been hard and he was hungry. He cut some wood from the forest; then he made a bow and arrow. He waited among the trees, beside the pool. At last a new animal came to drink at the pool. It was a soft, brown animal with large eyes and a crown on its head. Okohorote carried it on his back. The first animal killed by man. He carried it up the long, long tunnel, back up to the sky. The first food from earth.

His family came to meet him: children, brothers, sisters, parents, neighbours, friends, relations. They all came to hear his story: to hear the story of the great hole in the sky. That night, they sat in a circle around Okohorote. They sat among the dark moon clouds. The moon sat behind them like a lamp.

'I have something to give you all,' he said. Then he gave each adult and child a piece of the animal to eat. They ate for some minutes, silently.

'Everything we eat is tasteless beside this!' said one.

'I'm sick to death of our cloud-cakes and sky-spaghetti. This is delicious!'

Delicious. A new experience. Man's first taste of meat.

'There are other things there too,' said Okohorote. 'There is food growing from the ground and from trees, fruits as big as my hands.'

In the morning, a long line of people waited by the tunnel.

'Okohorote, take us down. Show us this new world.'

At first Okohorote was angry.

'One journey by one man is enough. Our life is here in the sky. That world below is for the birds and animals.'

'We want to see it too. Sky world is pleasant, but it's too quiet.'

'Yes,' said a young boy. 'I know everything about life here. I want to learn something new.'

'Okohorote,' said a sky-woman. 'You are jealous. You want that world for yourself. Well, we want to see it too.'

It was true. Okohorote wanted it to be his own private world. He had found it. It was his world. But he understood the sky-woman. It was their world too.

'Very well. Follow me, down the tunnel.'

He led the way. He showed them how to sit in the

tunnel and walk down. First Okohorote, then his friends, his brothers and sisters, his parents and grandparents, his neighbours and their children.

A long long line of people entering the new world. A place with more food, more riches, more colours and sounds.

The earth did not disappoint them. They found all the riches there they wanted. They also found the birds that had visited them before. Birds of every head, back, wing and song. The home of the birds and animals became their own home. None of them ever returned to the sky.

Chapter 5

How Death came to Earth

A myth of the Masai people of Kenya

'Mwalimu my teacher, a lion came to our fire with a child. It was a new lion, a new child in our forest. The next day I saw the new lion again. It was dead. Its eyes were white and open. There was blood on its neck. Mwalimu, who is god of our forest? Is it Life or is it Death? Why did the child-lion die?'

The teacher was quiet. He looked into the earth. For a long time he said nothing. They heard only the cry of birds and laughter of baboons from far away in the forest.

'The forest is good but also bad. How can this be?' he said. This is the story he told. 'For you, a child, this cannot be. When the world was a child, it was good. There was no death. All that lived, lived for always. Life had no end. At that time, only one man lived. His name was Kintu. He alone knew the laugh of baboons, the cry of the birds, the sun on the water. He knew them, without end, without death. But his time was short.

Other eyes were looking at him. They were the eyes of

Ngaysha, daughter to Ngai the first Maker. She was in the sky.

'Oh, father,' she said. 'It is so depressing in the sky. I detest it. Here I have only my brothers to talk to. Their sense of humour is appalling and they laugh at me all the time. I'm sick of them and sick of being here. I want something intelligent and interesting to do.'

'Look at that great earth below, Ngaysha. That is something intelligent and interesting to do. Study it well; there is nothing it cannot teach you.'

Ngaysha studied the earth. The birds taught her to sing. The baboons taught her to laugh. The rivers taught her to dance. Then she saw Kintu.

'Oh man that walks on earth, I was asleep until I saw you. The earth teaches me to sing, to laugh, to dance. But you teach my heart to fly. You teach me to love.'

Kintu was a new earth in her heart. Kintu was a dancing river for her. He was the song of the birds. Ngaysha went to her father.

'Father, the earth did indeed teach me everything. I studied it well. So well that I want the earth to be my home and the earth-man to be at the centre of it. Let this earth-man be my husband.'

Ngai was angry.

'Did I make the earth for this? Did I show you this earth, only to lose you?'

'Oh Father, you must let me go. In your home I am a child. In your home I am asleep. I must find a home for

myself. If you give me the earth-man, you give me life
itself.'

Ngai was not happy. But he understood her words.

'Very well. But this earth-man must come to our home.
Before he is your husband, I must know him well. I must
be sure he is a good man.'

Next day, Ngaysha went with the sunlight down to
earth. She sat by the water and waited for Kintu to come.

Kintu was walking through the trees. He walked
quietly; he did not want the animals to be afraid. He
walked without sound, like the wind. He knew the forest
well; he knew every leaf and tree; every bird and flower.
But he could feel something new in the air today. He
could see a new colour by the water and a new sound, like
laughing.

'Is there a new bird by the water?' he thought.

And then he came to the water. He came to the water
and saw Ngaysha.

She sat in the tall grass. Her head was bent, like a flower
drinking from the pool. Her hair fell like a bright river on
her back.

'Oh golden bird of the forest! Until now I saw nothing
so beautiful! Where were you until this moment? How
did I live until this moment?'

Ngaysha looked at him and laughed.

'You see me every night in the stars. You know me
without knowing. You see me every day in the sunlight,
and in the clouds. You see me without seeing.'

'Beautiful golden bird, show me what I did not see before.'

'Come with me to my home, Kintu earth-man. Come with me and I will give you new eyes.'

Kintu and Ngaysha went with the sunlight back to the sky. The winds in the sky blew and blew: the sky was dark with anger that day.

Kintu fought the winds. But they were stronger than all the lions in the forest. They pushed and blew and screamed.

'Stay by me Kintu earth-man! Do not be afraid!' cried Ngaysha.

And then the winds died. The sun moved higher in the sky. It was bright. It was so bright. The light was like a knife to Kintu.

'I cannot see! Help me! Help me! I cannot see!' he cried. The sun burned him and cut him: it cut his face like the claws of a cat.

'Stay by me Kintu earth-man! Do not be afraid!' cried Ngaysha.

And then the sun became quieter. Kintu's body hurt: every part of it hurt. But he stayed with Ngaysha. The clouds moved quietly, slowly. Kintu walked into the cloud. The cloud filled his eyes, his ears, his mouth. The cloud filled his lungs.

'I cannot breathe! Help me! Help me! I cannot breathe!' he cried.

'Stay by me Kintu earth-man! Do not be afraid!' said Ngaysha.

And then the clouds moved away. Kintu was standing before the house of Ngai.

Ngai came to meet him.

'Welcome Kintu earth-man! You are a good man, fine and true. You have passed every test. You stayed with Ngaysha, even when you were afraid. You stayed, even when it was dangerous. You are the man that can love my daughter. With you she will be happy. You will be a true husband as she will be a true wife.'

Kintu laughed and cried together.

'How can I thank you? How can I show you how happy I am?' he said.

'By listening to my words,' said Ngai. 'Now Kintu, I will give you gifts to take to earth: chickens, that will give you eggs; goats, that will give you milk; corn and beans and nuts for you to eat. You will not be hungry. Your children will not be hungry. Use these gifts well, and you will be happy.'

In the morning, Ngaysha and Kintu were married. The wind kissed them, the birds sang for them, the sun built them a road of light. Kintu was so happy, he forgot the time.

'Kintu dear husband,' said Ngaysha, 'we must go. Soon the road will be too dark to travel.'

Kintu and Ngaysha quickly made themselves ready. Ngai made himself ready too. He came to the gate of his house with them.

'Oh daughter, I want to be happy as I send you on your road. But half of me is lost when you go away.'

'Father, do not be sad. You have not lost me, I am always your daughter. But we must hurry. Every moment it is darker.'

'Before you go, listen to me, Kintu and Ngaysha. Your brother Death does not know of this wedding. When angry, he is terrible. You must never return on this road. This road must be closed to you forever. Remember this, dear children. There must be no return.'

'We must go! Goodbye, goodbye father!' And Kintu and Ngaysha disappeared into the dark. Ngai walked into his house. The house was very empty and very dark.

Husband and wife travelled for many hours. The road was long and dark. Kintu felt tired. The goats dropped their heads: the chickens jumped and danced.

'Ngaysha, let us stop a while. I am tired and hungry. The chickens and goats are tired and hungry.'

'Yes, dear husband. Let us eat some of the food my father gave us.'

Kintu opened the bag he was carrying. He put his hand into the bag.

'I can feel the nuts here in the bag.'

'Can you feel the beans?'

'Yes, the beans are here.'

'Can you feel the corn?'

'I can feel the nuts. I can feel the beans. But there is no corn.'

Kintu put his whole arm into the bag, up to the shoulder. But still he could find no corn.

'No corn?! No corn, Kintu my husband? Are you sure? Let me try.'

Ngaysha also put her whole arm into the bag. She put her head into the bag, until she almost disappeared.

'No corn! No corn for the chickens!'

'Oh Ngaysha, oh my wife. We hurried away so fast, I left the corn in the sky. Ngaysha, I have left the best gift behind.'

Ngaysha looked at him.

'It is not important, Kintu my husband. We can eat the beans.'

'Wait for me here, Ngaysha. I will be a short time away. No, do not stop me.'

'Oh Kintu, don't leave me. Don't walk again on the road of no return.'

'With you in my heart, the journey will be fast. Wait for me.'

He pushed her away. And then he disappeared on the road of no return.

Ngaysha sat among the goats and chickens. She cried until her face burned. The goats put their heads in the bag, and ate. They ate and ate like hungry children. They ate, and Ngaysha cried, and the chickens jumped. And so it was, for hour after hour after hour.

At last when light came, Kintu arrived. He carried with him a bag of corn. He and Ngaysha held each other for a

long time. They held each other with no words. There was
a darkness on their shoulders. Then they walked to earth;
Ngaysha, Kintu, the goats, the chickens, the bags of corn
and beans. And behind them, quietly, slowly, darkly,
walked another. Quiet, slow, dark. He followed behind,
each step exactly following the one before. Their steps
made his road. They could not see him. They could only
feel his darkness. And he followed them to earth. And
there he stayed, and waited.

One day, Ngaysha walked to the water alone. It was the
place where she and Kintu first met. She sat by the water
and bent her head.

'Our life is so happy. We have beautiful children. Our
home is beautiful. Our love is strong and true after many
years. But I feel a darkness in the forest. I feel afraid. For
so many years, this darkness has not left me. And I don't
know why.'

And then she felt a hand on her shoulder. It was as cold
as ice. It was as heavy as stone. She could not move.

'I am your brother Death. You left me without saying
goodbye. I came to find you.'

Ngaysha could not speak. The words died in her
mouth.

'Your husband Kintu showed me the road. That was
very kind of him. And now I like it so much here on earth,
I think I will stay.'

Ngaysha could not speak. The words died in her
mouth.

Kintu found her one hour later. She was still warm. She sat in the tall grass. Her head was bent like a flower drinking from the pool. Her hair fell like a bright river on her back.

'Oh golden bird of the forest. You taught my eyes to see. You taught my heart to fly. How can I live now without you, with only Death as my friend?'

And so Death became Master over the Earth.'

And now the story of the new lion in the forest became clear.

'Oh Mwalimu. So that is why the child-lion died. How can I live with Death as master in the forest?'

'Know this. The good things in the forest came from love. They came from Ngai the father: his love for Ngaysha, her love for Kintu. Remember the good things. Their price is very high. For those great and good things, the price was Death.'

'I am afraid, still, my teacher.'

'Know this. For one bad thing there are a thousand, a million good things. Walk in peace my son.'

Chapter 6

The Great Flood

Myth of the Inca People of Peru

On the highest mountain above Urubamba is a city of stone. It hangs like a great bird over the valley below. It hangs as if dropped from the sky and spreads walls and streets like stone wings. From the mountain top, you can see green valleys fall away on all sides: you can see circles of houses, village fires, thick forest baking in the sun. In one of the fields behind the village, a man and an animal are walking. They walk slowly; every few minutes the animal stops; the man stops. The man pulls at the rope; the animal holds its ground, pulls its head away. Then they move again, slowly.

'Oh Llama what is the matter with you. You hang your head. You pull away. You show me these sad eyes. Why do you not eat this rich good grass? Is it not the best grass of all?'

The llama lifted its head and looked at the man. The man saw the animal's eyes as clearly as if they spoke. They were dark. Above all, they were afraid.

'You are so afraid!' he said. 'Why? Are there bad animals near? No? Bad men? Are you sick? Are you dying?'

Coto looked into the intelligent eyes again.

'What are you telling me, Llama? You are telling me that I am dying? That we are all dying. That all living things are dying?'

Llama turned its eyes to the sea, then back to Coto, and hung its head.

'The sea. You are telling me it is the sea. The sea will leave its bed. It will cover the earth and we will all die. Oh llama can this be! Do I understand you?'

Llama looked at him: a long, cold look.

'Yes, I do understand. This will be.'

Coto could not speak. He felt ice in his blood. He stood and looked at the world. The blue mountains lost in cloud: the fields bright in the sun: the roofs of huts among the trees. He heard children from the village laughing.

'All this must go?' he said.

Llama pulled at his rope. He pulled and shook his head. His legs pulled them towards the village.

'And there is no time to stand. No time to look. We must hurry. Tell me Llama. How long is there? One year? One month? One week? Less? Less than all this?!'

Then they were running to the village; Llama running, Coto pulling behind. Running, shouting, crying 'Five days! Only five days!'

They ran to Coto's hut. Like a mad man Coto dashed around his hut. All the food he found he put in a basket. Enough food for five days. Llama ran round and round the hut. He lifted clouds of dust. Coto turned over pots full of milk and flour. Bananas, nuts, coconuts, pots of honey and flour, bread, corn; he threw them all into the basket.

Llama was waiting at the door when he finished. He turned his head to the mountains. Coto took the rope and followed.

The journey was long and hard. The sun burned down. Above the forest there was nowhere to escape from the sun. The basket became heavier and heavier. It cut into Coto's hands like a knife. And the path climbed higher and higher: village and forest dropped below. The huts and trees became as small as flies.

'How much farther?' cried Coto.

He only wanted the journey to end. He could feel only the ice in his blood, and the sun on his head.

Llama looked at him with eyes so cold they frightened him.

'You think escape is easy?' they said. The eyes laughed at him, with animal coldness.

Coto threw a coconut out of the basket. That made the basket lighter. Then they continued on the path. The sun came and went. Night fell over them four times. At last Llama's walk slowed down. And then the hot dusty path finished. There, at the path's end, jumping and twisting, laughing and chatting, was every animal under the sun. Every animal known to Coto. Every friend, enemy and relation of Llama. A sea of colour: red, gold, green, silver of birds wings, goats' beards, horses' tails, foxes' backs.

Coto looked at Llama.

'Yes. All the animals knew,' said the eyes of Llama.

'And I am the only man,' thought Coto. He thought of the children in the village, the old men in the fields, the women by the river, the boys running and playing in the forest.

'All this must go?' he said.

A crash like a volcano erupting took his words away. The sea was moving forward in great sheets. Sheet on sheet on sheet covered the valleys below. It hunted out every corner of the valley: washing over the roofs of huts, the tops of trees. Rivers opened out and ran with the sea. The world was a flat table of water.

'All this must go?' cried Coto.

The water moved like a bowl of boiling soup. It moved and climbed: higher and higher the water climbed. And it boiled and broke against the mountains. The animals hurried together, to the highest part of the mountain. The animals stood, hundreds of them, all squeezed together. And the sea crashed against the mountain: great tongues of water twisted around them. And the soup boiled nearer, nearer, nearer.

'We too must go?' cried Coto.

Llama looked at him. His eyes were clear, quiet. They said, 'No. Not us. We are the ones that must live. We are the ones that must make a new world.'

'How can I make a new world? I cannot forget the old one.'

Llama looked at him again with that animal coldness. 'Then you must forget.'

At last the water stopped. The world was a still silver sheet. The clouds moved in it. The sun came and went in it. A flat plate of water. Only the mountain top broke the flatness. The animals stood so close: the nose of the cat beside the foot of the bear, the back of the fox under the chin of the llama, and Coto between them all. Then the water began to fall. Slowly, quietly, the water fell. New mountain tops appeared. The mountains lifted like washed blue islands out of the water. The water washed down the mountain walls. It slipped and twisted and ran back into the valleys. The sheets of water pulled back to their bed. Valleys, fields and villages lay uncovered. Coto looked at his old land. Trees were thrown into the fields. Last tongues of water ran among the broken huts. And there was a terrifying silence below.

'Why was I the only man to live?' he asked. 'It was not my choice.'

There was work to make a new world. On the mountain top, new people were made. They were painted all colours: they were made big and small, they were made with long and short hair, with round and long eyes, dark and fair skin, tall, short, wide and narrow.

The work was nearly complete. The sun was high, over the valleys. Below, the land was dry again and the sea was quiet. Trees stood tall again and fields of grass moved in the wind. The birds flew again. They sat in the trees and sang. Fox, horse, goat, pig, walked back to the valleys.

One day, a bird flew into the tree beside Coto. The bird was as white as a moon. It sat in the tree and spread its wings. It sat among the leaves like a fallen star, and sang. Coto stopped his work.

'I have made people. I have made enough people for a new world. But I cannot give them life. You are smaller than my hand but you have more life than all of them.'

The bird looked at Coto and sang.

'I will give them life! I will give them words, songs, languages!'

And he blew language on the wind. Words and songs blew from his mouth into theirs, and the air became filled with sound. Laughing, singing, talking, crying, shouting. Coto ran among the new people. He looked into one man's face: a wonderful face, with bright teeth and eyes, with wide bones and wide smile.

'Salaam!' said the man.

'I don't understand this,' said Coto.

Then another, and another, and another. Wonderful faces, sad and smiling, laughing and serious, cheerful and miserable.

'But not one word do I understand!' said Coto.

Then he found Llama. Llama's eyes looked at him.

'These are new people; for every tongue a new tongue.'

'This was not in the old world,' said Coto.

Llama's eyes were cold.

'Then you must forget the old world.'

He turned, and walked away. He walked down the mountain, back to the valleys.

Machu Pichu, city of stone, sits on the highest mountain above Urubamba. It hangs like a great bird over the valley below. From the mountain top, you can see green valleys fall away on all sides; you can see circles of homes, village fires, thick forests baking in the sun. Here it was that mankind escaped from the great flood, and where mankind walked again back into the valleys and filled the world with many tongues.

Chapter 7

Magic Islands: the Irish Watermen

Celtic myth of Irish heroes

There are men who travel the sea forever. From time to time their boats come near to land, then they pull away again. They sit on the sea at night. The seals lie on the rocks, seagulls circle and cry above their heads. Sometimes they sing to make time pass. Sometimes they spread their nets in the water and draw in a crowd of fish.

Their boats have circled the world, every sea and ocean north, south, east and west. They have seen the smoke of volcanoes rise above the sea. They have seen strange sea-animals moving above the water.

Bran and his friends once lived on the coast of Ireland. They once lived where green hills fell to the sea, where fields lay washed with rain. They knew the people of the villages, and the village people knew them.

One day, many years ago, Bran was spreading his nets out on the sand to dry. It was November, and the wind was fierce and cold. Bran worked, bent over the nets. The wind pushed and pulled at the nets. It blew sand and salt into his face and eyes. Then suddenly it touched him on the shoulder. The touch was gentle, light as a lover's. He

looked. A woman stood beside him. Her eyes were ice-blue: they laughed at him, as he fought below with the nets. This was no village woman. Her skin was white as ice, as if she had never known wind and sun. She wore no shoes, but had walked over the sands and rocks with no injury. Bran looked, his mouth wide with surprise.

'Bran, silly man. Look at you. Tonight you will go back to your home. You will spend the evening in the pub. You'll come home drunk. Then you'll go to sleep, and wake up tired. What sort of life is that?'

No words came to Bran. His mouth was as dry as an oven.

'You can do better than that. There are whole worlds out there.' She threw her long white arm out to the sea. Though the wind cut like ice, her arms were bare.

'Aren't . . . you cold?' Bran said at last. Her laugh was like glass breaking.

'The sea will give you more than all this. It will give you things you only dreamed of before.'

Bran looked to sea. Things he had only dreamed of before appeared on the water. Islands with no rain, strange sea-animals, coastlines of boiling mountains, castles and temples, and more women as beautiful as this one.

When he turned to her again, she had gone. Bran stood up. He shook his head. He rubbed his eyes. Was this a dream? Am I drunk? Am I sick? The wind blew and covered her footprints with sand.

'Come to sea with me,' he asked Mael his friend. 'You will find things there you only dreamed of before.'

'I don't want that, Bran,' Mael said. 'My Sandra will miss me. What will my children do without me?'

'We will only be a short time. We will be back by morning.'

'That cannot be. Dreams take more than a day to find.'

'Come on man. Are you afraid? There are whole new worlds out there.'

'Ay Bran true enough. But I'm right happy here, with this one.'

'Think of the stories you'll have to tell, man. Think of the presents you can bring home.'

They met by the sea wall. It was not yet morning. The darkness sat like a coat of salt on their skin. They pushed the boats out to sea. The boats left two deep cuts in the sand. They pushed until the boats lifted on the water. Then they were away. The boats moved away with the tide. Bran cut the water with his paddle. Right, left, right, left: the water moved with him. It fell away on either side as the boat forced a route through the dark.

'What are you dreaming of, Mael Duin?' asked Bran.

The paddle cut Mael's hands until they bled. The wind cut his face and brought tears to his eyes.

'That I am home, Bran. That I am in a field of flowers, sheep around me, fruit trees all around. The sun shining.'

The sun came up above the line of water. They moved through the half-light and half-sea. They saw water and fields of flowers, fish and jumping lambs. Their dreams spread themselves over the sea.

And then a line of land moved towards them.

'This is what I wanted!' Bran shouted.

'Let's visit quickly, then go back,' Mael said. They paddled their boats to the beach. The trees had the smell of sweet wine. Even the smell made Bran drunk.

The woman with ice-blue eyes was waiting for them. Her skin was as white as ice.

'Good, Bran. You have done well. And Mael Duin too.'

She took Mael's hand and helped him from the boat.

'Do you know me?' he said.

She laughed. Her laugh was like ice breaking.

'She is too beautiful to be good,' Mael thought. 'I wish Sandra was here.'

The ice-woman led Mael across the beach. They walked through the trees into the hills. Mael's steps were slow and heavy at first. But the trees sent out their smell of sweet wine. And the hand holding his was so soft. And the distant sea made so sleepy a song. His steps became lighter.

For one year Mael Duin forgot. And Bran was happy. Not for one moment did Bran miss his home. But then, after one year, Mael's dreams changed. He dreamt again of fields of flowers, a path of fruit trees, his house at the end of the path, Sandra in his house, waiting by the fire.

'I must go back, Bran. Sandra is waiting.'

'That she won't be, Mael Duin,' said Bran. 'She'll be off by now.'

'Then I must go back and find her. I have learnt everything of this island. There is no more to learn. I want to go home.'

At first Bran laughed at Mael Duin. But every day he talked of home. One day, the ice-woman did too.

'Bran, it is time for you to leave. You are lazy and drunk all the time. You live only for amusement. It is time for you to have other dreams.'

They walked back to the beaches. The boats were still there, as they had left them. The paddles lay ready for them. The woman with ice-blue eyes stood by the boats.

'Your feet must never touch land again,' she said. 'If they do, they will make just one footprint.'

Mael and Bran pushed their boats along the sand. The boats lifted, moved with the water. They dropped their paddles and moved out with the tide. They were on the open sea for many days. The sea was grey and cold. Mael Duin dreamt of home, the fishing nets and the village pub again, the open fire, his children, Sandra.

'Really, Mael, can home be the same again? When we've seen all this, done all this. Is home what it was?'

'I learnt nothing Bran. I learnt only what I had left behind.'

The boats fought the winds, and climbed the high water. The sun rose and fell, rose and fell. And then a line of land moved towards them. It was the land they knew. The clouds sat in the hills, and wet sands fell out into the sea. The rocks were bright with rain.

A fisherman bent over his nets on the beach. The wind pulled and fought. It climbed into his shirt and blew it out like a balloon.

'This is a pig of a wind, right enough,' he said.

Bran and Mael Duin moved nearer.

'Throw us a rope will you, man,' shouted Bran.

The fisherman stood up. He ran out to meet them.

'Where are you from, then?' he shouted.

'We are Bran and Mael Duin from this village here.'

'Well, I know no-one of that name,' he said. 'The only Bran of these parts was that one of old times long gone.'

'Who was that then?' asked Bran.

'Well, history tells of a fisherman from these parts. One day he went to sea. Never came back. No living thing saw him again. But they say he travelled the seas. He saw the like of none before him.'

'They say that, do they?'

'Oh they do. Grand stories they tell of that Bran and Mael Duin.'

'How long ago was that, old man?'

'Oh, time before any of us knew. Time of history it was, when the town was but a village.'

'The town?'

'Ay.'

Bran could hear cold laughter in the wind. 'Just one footprint,' she said.

Mael Duin pulled at the rope. The wind laughed around his ears.

'I am going,' he shouted. The wind carried his words away. Threw them into the air.

'I can't stay in this boat.'

Bran held his arm.

'Are you a madman?'

'Yes! Mad! Mad until I am home again.'

Then Mael half stepped, half fell from the boat. His foot touched the sand. It made one footprint.

The wind blew and covered him with sand. Bran's boat pulled out again to sea. The seagulls circled above his head.

Glossary

arrow   a long thin object used to hurt or kill

baboon   a monkey that lives in Africa

basket   a bag made of dry grass

blind   unable to see

bow   a long piece of wood with horsehair across it, made for shooting arrows

branch   a part of a tree where leaves, flowers and fruit grow

claw   the long sharp toes of a cat

climb   to move upwards

companion   a friend

corn   the seed from plants, from which bread and flour can be made

crack   a very narrow break, as narrow as a hair

crawl   to move on hands and feet, very low on the ground

crown   a marvellous tall hat like a king or queen wears

deer

fierce   very strong, angry and violent
grow   to become bigger
hut   a small house
lamb

lion   a large cat, king of the cat family, living in Africa
net   a bag of strong ropes, used to catch fish
paddle   a long flat object, used to move a small boat
palm   the palm of a hand is the inside part of the hand
peace   opposite of war
pool   a small place of still water
shadow   a dark place where the sunlight cannot go
skin   the outside cover of an animal or person
snake

suffer   to feel pain and worry
tobacco   the leaves which are smoked in cigarettes
toy   objects children play with
valley   the low land between hills or mountains
vine   a plant that climbs and grows fruit that makes wine

waves   the movement sea water makes, because of tides and winds
wings   the part a bird or aeroplane uses to fly
yolk   the yellow part inside an egg

Glossary of Names

Atlantis   an island believed to be lost under the sea
Arthur   a king and hero of Britain in Celtic stories
Avalon   the island where Arthur travelled after death
Bran   an Irish sea-traveller who travelled to strange islands
Coxcotli   the woman in the Aztec story, who lived after the flood
Machu Pichu   a city of the Incas, in the Andes of Peru. The Incas believed man was remade here after the great flood
Mael Duin   an Irish sea-traveller who visited thirty-one islands
Morgan la Fay   the sister of Arthur and priestess of water
Mwalimu   the word for 'teacher' in the language of east Africa, Swahili
Ngai   the name for the Maker, for the Masai people of northern Kenya

Noah the man in the Bible story who lived after the flood

Okohorote the first man to find the earth, in the story of the Warau people

Papatua the Maori name for the earth

Rangi the Maori name for the sky

Sedi-Diyor the man who pushed the sky away from earth in the Minyong Indian story

Tangaloa (or Tangaroa) the highest god in the Polynesian islands

Villca-Coto the mountain 70 miles north of Cuzco, where man escaped the great flood

Xowalaci the Giver and Maker in the creation story of the Joshua people